Vigil

Vigil

Morris Panych

Talonbooks
1996

Published with the assistance of the Canada Council.

The author extends special thanks to Urjo Kareda.

Talonbooks
P.O. Box 2076, Vancouver, British Columbia, Canada V6B 3S3
www.talonbooks.com

Typeset in New Baskerville and Frutiger and printed and bound in
Canada.

Third Printing: July 2008

Library and Archives Canada Cataloguing in Publication

Panych, Morris.
  Vigil

  A play.
  ISBN 0-88922-365-3

  I. title.
PS8581.A65V53 1996   C812'.54   C96-910509-6
PR9199.3.P325V53 1996

ISBN-10: 0-88922-365-3
ISBN-13: 978-0-88922-365-3

For John Moffat

Vigil was first produced as a co-operative venture between the Belfry Theatre of Victoria, B.C., and the Arts Club Theatre of Vancouver, B.C., opening first at the Belfry Theatre on September 28, 1995, and subsequently at the Arts Club Theatre on October 28, 1995, with the following cast:

GRACE .... Margaret Barton

KEMP .... Alan Williams

Directed by Morris Panych
Set and Costume Design by Ken MacDonald
Lighting Design by Marsha Sibthorpe
Sound Design by Ian Rye
Stage Managers: Dorothy Rogers (Victoria)
Louis-Marie Bournival (Vancouver)

Vigil also opened at the Tarragon Theatre in Toronto, Ontario on December 27, 1995, with the following cast:

GRACE .... Joyce Campion

KEMP .... Brian Tree

Directed by Morris Panych
Set and Costume Design by Ken MacDonald
Lighting Design by Bonnie Beecher
Sound Design by Ian Rye
Stage Manager: Cheryl Francis

ACT ONE
SCENE ONE

In darkness, a doorbell. Music. Lights up on a mantle clock, ticking. Lights up on an upstairs room in a decrepit old house. GRACE sits up in her bed looking at KEMP who stands near the door, battered suitcase in hand. A long pause, as KEMP looks about uncomfortably.

KEMP:
Yes. Well.

He puts down the suitcase.

I didn't expect you to be pleased to see me. Hardly anybody ever is.

GRACE throws a hairbrush at him. Pause. Music. Blackout.

Scene Two

As before, KEMP standing beside his suitcase.
GRACE in bed. Music tails out.

KEMP:

I got your letter. I didn't know what to make
of it. I read things far too quickly to ever
understand them. 'Old and dying' looks very
much like 'yodeling' when you run it all
together like that. [*Pause*] I didn't know you
were still alive. I dropped everything. Took
the train a thousand miles. Got here just as
fast as I could. I hailed a cab at the station.
Handed the driver my bag and told him to
step on it. [*Pause*] I was in...such a hurry. It's
been a long time. A long...time. You look...my
goodness, well, you weren't exaggerating. No.
And me...well, me. I really haven't changed
all that much. I've got those little bits of skin
that stick out here and there, under my arms
and such, but otherwise, no. I haven't
changed much at all. [*Pause*] Sorry.

GRACE draws the blanket up over her head.
Blackout.

Scene Three

*Later. KEMP, seated on his suitcase near
GRACE. She is still hidden.*

KEMP:
　　Let's not talk about anything depressing,
　　alright? [*Pause*] Do you want to be cremated?

　　GRACE peeks out from her blanket. Blackout.

Scene Four

Daylight. KEMP is seated at the window, looking out at the rain. GRACE sits, staring straight ahead. He turns to look at her. He looks at his watch. Looks at her again. Looks out the window.

KEMP:

There's this woman across the street who's been sitting in her window, staring at me for about three hours now. Don't people have anything better to do with their lives? Oh, that's right. Now I remember. They don't. [*Coming away from the window, looking at his watch*] It's been three days. And my pants are getting wrinkled. What am I supposed to wear to your service?

Blackout.

Scene Five

Night. More rain. KEMP sits on his suitcase, sleeping. GRACE watches. She gets out of bed with her cane and moves towards him. She pokes him with the cane. KEMP wakes suddenly. He looks at GRACE. Looks at his watch. Looks at her again. She returns to her bed as the lights fade to black.

SCENE SIX

GRACE stands at the door. Hearing KEMP,
she scuttles back to bed. KEMP enters with a
tray of food.

KEMP:

We should discuss your organs. [*He serves*
food, cutting it into pieces, as she watches] I
thought you might be interested in donating
something to the cause of science, although I
can't imagine what. Fine. I'll let you think
about it. But don't think for too long. Unless
you've signed the forms they can't touch you.
Well, otherwise they'd be stripping people for
parts, like cars. Please don't salt that before
you even taste it. That's very annoying.
[*Taking salt away*] This isn't a restaurant. Why
do you always look at me like that? Alright, so
I didn't visit you for thirty years. I was busy.
[*Salting her food, wildly*] Here! Have some salt!
Happy? [*Lightly*] Why do you hate me so
much? I'm your nephew for God's sake. Is it
too much to ask, just to pretend? [*He cries for*
a second and then recovers] I'm sorry. I'm sorry.
It's just that the longer you stay alive—I mean
—not that you should die, but the more you
get to know me, it seems, the worse I get.
[*Pause*] Alright. Fine. You don't have to like
me.

14

He sticks meat onto a fork and presents it to her.

But you'd bloody-well better like my cooking.

GRACE turns her head away. Blackout.

Scene Seven

*Later, KEMP, feather duster in hand, and
wearing a handkerchief over his face, cleans the
room, as GRACE watches.*

KEMP:

Right. I'm just going to sort through your
things. I thought we'd have one of those
estate auctions. We probably won't get much,
but it'll cover the expenses anyway. You'd be
surprised what an urn can cost these days.
What's wrong? I have to wear this. I'm sensi-
tive to dust. Ever since I arrived here, you've
been behaving as if I was committing some
sort of crime. I resent that. I know I haven't
been the best relation in the world, but I'm
all you have left. And I'd really appreciate it if
you didn't act so suspicious of me all the
time. Here. [*Producing a document*] Sign your
will. You're leaving everything to me.

Blackout.

SCENE EIGHT

GRACE, alone, is out of bed and looking into KEMP's empty suitcase. Hearing KEMP approach, she shuts the case, and scuttles back to bed. He enters with a tray of food. Stops. Looks at suitcase. Looks at her.

KEMP:

I spoke to a funeral director today. You don't mind recorded music, do you? Of course not. I don't mean this in a cruel way, but practically speaking, you're the only one who won't have to listen to it. I took the liberty of choosing something for you. Don't worry. It's quite sad. [*Pause; starts to cry*] I'm sorry. I'm sorry. It's just the thought of how moved I'll be when I hear it. Oh dear. [*Recovering, he takes out a measuring tape, and begins to measure her as she eats*] I had a lovely idea about the ashes, by the way. I thought I might mix you in with some soil and plant an Amaryllis. Would you like that? [*Off her look*] What's wrong with you? It's a perfectly enchanting notion. [*Taking the tray away*] I think you've eaten enough. [*Pause as they eye each other*] You'll never fit into the box.

Blackout.

Scene Nine

*KEMP, looking out the window. GRACE, in
bed, as before, knitting.*

KEMP:

Look at her. Still sitting there. Who's her taxi-
dermist, I wonder. [*Pause*] My God, it's
Spring. [*Watching below*] You ought to see this
poor man limping through the slush. [*He
laughs a little, turning back into the room*]
Spring. [*Pause*] I used to love this season
when I was a kid. I didn't have to skate anymore. You can't imagine what that looked
like. I had a pair of white lace-ups. And a
little white muff. I was so unhappy. Not
because I looked like a girl. But because I
wasn't one. I won't explain that. I never
skated, of course. I just skidded around like
Bambi. Or stood at the side, with the snow
coming down all around, watching these
parents pushing their precious children
along the ice, and wishing it would all
just...melt.

I hated winter. For different reasons than I
hate it now, of course. I'm not sure why I
hate it now. There's just something about the
sheer density of it. Not the cold. I love the
cold. No. I suppose it's the way people hud-
dle together in masses. Surviving on their
own sickening warmth. If you look out over

18

the city in the wintertime, you can actually
see it breathe. Like a strange sort of hibernat-
ing beast. Lying there, dreaming of Spring,
and grinding its teeth. [*Pause; change of mood*]
By the way. What should I do with your den-
tures?

Blackout.

SCENE TEN

*Night. KEMP sleeps in a chair. GRACE
watches him. She knits by the light from the
window. She stops. Studies KEMP for a
moment. Puts her knitting down very carefully,
and slowly gets out of bed. She tiptoes past
KEMP towards a cupboard. She gets a drop-
cloth. She goes to KEMP and covers him like a
piece of furniture. She returns to her bed, and
begins knitting again. He looks out from the
cloth. Wonders. Tucks it under his chin.
Sleeps. Fade to black.*

Scene Eleven

*KEMP stands before GRACE with a candle
and some matches. GRACE watches, knitting.*

KEMP:

I enter. The music is playing. [*He plays a
record on an old portable player*] Everyone is
seated. The mood is very somber, but upbeat.
You had a good long life. That's all anybody
can ask for. I light the candle. [*He lights the
candle*] It's a metaphor. I compare you to this
candle, melting. How it burns itself down
into a kind of coagulated lump at the
bottom. That's your body. But your spirit is
the light from the flame, and when the wax is
gone, the spirit...the spirit...[*He starts to cry,
but recovers*] I'm sorry, I was suddenly just
so...transported by that image. Well, what's
wrong? I have to compare you to something.
You don't exactly inspire the literary mind,
you know. Sitting there all day eating butterscotch pudding and going to the bathroom.
I'm sorry, but there's only so much that can
be said about that. Do you want people to cry
or not? Fine. Write your own eulogy. I've got
better things to do. [*Ending the music, he takes
the record and smashes it*] Now look what you've
done. [*Pause, and then off-handedly*] I don't
even know why I came here in the first place.
I left my job. Did you know that? Of course
not. But I quit my job to come here. I had a

21

very important position with a very important bank. Alright, not a very important position. And not a very important bank. But I left all the same. And I don't think it's too much of an exaggeration to say that I was accomplished. I had friends. Alright, acquaintances. Lots of them. I was somebody. I didn't live in this stupid town anymore. I was urbane. Witty. Understand? Well, perhaps not witty, but I was droll, alright? I ate in restaurants where they serve things you wouldn't even dream of eating. Portions so tiny that nobody ever even went to the bathroom. Do you understand? And when people died, which wasn't very often in my circle, they had the decency to disappear into a hospital, and anaesthetize themselves into oblivion, saving the rest of us the excruciating discomfort of having to participate. [*Pause; he cleans up the broken record*] And please don't take that the wrong way. Of course I want to be here. In the first place, it's my duty. In the second place...well, let's just say it's my duty and leave it at that. I'm not one of these types who abdicates their responsibility. I certainly have no intention of dumping you onto the state. I don't believe in that. You're my problem. And I don't mean problem, of course. You know what I mean. Fine. If you don't want to be compared to a candle, fine. [*Pause; he tosses the pieces into a waste basket*] In fact, maybe you're right. Why on earth should we compare ourselves to anything? I

loathe metaphors anyway. What a stupid idea.
You're not a candle. You're an old woman
with dirty hair. If you were a candle, well.

*KEMP wets his fingers and snuffs out the
candle. Blackout.*

SCENE TWELVE

*KEMP sits, trying to read a book on **How To Grieve**, flipping through the pages haphazardly, as GRACE knits.*

KEMP:

Not one picture of me. Not one. In all of your things there is not one single picture of me! As a matter of fact, there isn't a picture of anybody. I can't blame you for disavowing my parents. Who wouldn't. But me? Why? For years I sent you a picture of myself. How could you just throw them all away? What about that one of me with the mumps? That was adorable. It's as if I never existed in your mind. This is unbearable. All those years that I thought you'd forgotten about me, you actually had! [*Pause*] This knitting of yours. [*Pause*] Is it a long-term project?

She continues to knit as he stares at her. He goes back to his book.

Blackout.

SCENE THIRTEEN

KEMP, up at the window, looking out.
GRACE, as before. She applies lipstick to her
lips and cheeks with the aid of a compact
mirror, which she also uses to watch KEMP.

KEMP:

I can't believe it's Summer already. And she's
still sitting there in that window. [*Pause*] Look
at those kids throwing that ball at each other.
They're going to break a bloody window.
How perfect if one of them should get hit on
the head. I much preferred the indoors when
I was a kid. I used to play for hours and
hours, with a portable hair-dryer hood. I put
it on so I could hear messages from outer
space, of course. I would explain to the aliens
my life at home. It wasn't easy. By the way,
I've got an infection in my throat. Don't
worry. It's probably just cancer of the esopha-
gus. Well, we all have to die of something,
don't we? I used to smoke, you know. I
looked ridiculous, but I did it anyway. I quit
smoking the day Mother died. I only did it to
annoy her. It wasn't easy to quit. I was quite
addicted to annoying her. [*Pause*] I put the
cigarette out in her ashes. [*Pause*] What
became of you, by the way, that you couldn't
even make the funeral? I may have been an
awful nephew, but you were a dreadful aunt. I
don't think you've ever sent me so much as a

birthday card. Except for this year. I didn't tell you, but I took the liberty of sending myself a birthday card. From you. Of course, it didn't arrive today. Why would it? Look. There he goes. The mailman brought nothing. Some things never change. [*Pause*] Look at those kids. One of them's going to chuck that thing right in front of a car. Why don't they know that? Maybe that's why I can't stand the little, barefooted creeps. They're so distressingly stupid. [*Sound of a car screeching to a halt*] Like little insane, drunken midgets. Running around, all over the street, smashing into each other. It's so depressing. Just to catch a stupid ball. Just watch one of them get conked on the head now. There he goes. Ha, ha! What did I tell you? Off to his mother, crying his stupid little head off. [*Pause*] Well, it's my birthday. I never dreamed I'd be spending it with you. Of course, I never dreamed I'd be spending it with anybody, but there you are. Very few people know that is the day I was born. It's not the kind of information I'd casually share with my friends, even if I had any. I suppose you're wondering how a person can go through life without accumulating a single friend, even inadvertently. Let me tell you, it isn't easy making yourself so resoundingly unpopular. You really have to work at it. Of course, I don't like people, so that's a good start, I suppose. It's not just that I can take them or leave them. I really don't like them.

26

Children, of course, are just a smaller, stickier variety; less apt to talk post-modernism, which is a large part of their charm. But real people —I mean adults—before they shrivel away and die that is, exude a kind of sickening...mist from their pores. Carbon dioxide, mixed with desperation. I can often smell it on an elevator. Disguised under all that rancid cologne, and stale cigarette smoke. Desperation. Lining up, crowding in. Pushing. People wanting, wanting. Desperately. To go. To pass. To cross. To enter. To live. To live! That's the thing that always gets me. People want so much to live. I saw that man again, yesterday, just over there, on the other side of the park, over there, limping along on his wooden leg. I tried to imagine the effort it must have taken him to get there. The physical pain of losing that limb, the interminable rehabilitation he must have undergone. The taunting of children. The personal anguish and torment. All so he could hobble across some park clutching his little bag of groceries? Why? Is life that important, that no suffering, no humiliation is too great? I wanted to just...push him over. [*Pause*] Well, at least it gives me a small degree of pleasure that people have such a fervent, tooth grinding...urgency about them. Otherwise, I really wouldn't have enjoyed working in a bank so much. As it was, I could make people wait an eternity. Until they turned to stone. Look at that woman pushing that pram. Imagine having your whole life ahead of you. Oh, that poor little creature. There's only one day I wish I could live over again. If I could. One perfect day. Beginning to end. I couldn't have been more than seven. I hid up in the attic with the cat. For the whole day. Eavesdropping into Mother's heart. I could hear her calling 'where's my baby?' and 'where did you get to, you little rascal'. Going from room to room. Looking everywhere. Within hours she was phoning friends and neighbours. 'Have you seen him?', and 'Do you think I should go look?' By evening, when Father came home, she was actually weeping. 'He hasn't returned! What if he's hurt?' I even cried a little to myself. And then they went out to search for me. When they were gone, I snuck down, and crept into my bed. I imagined them finding me. What joy on their faces to see me fast asleep. Their darling boy. Safe from harm. And the vows between them to be better parents. To love me more from now on. And never to let me out of their sight again. They were the sweetest dreams I think I ever had. When I woke in the morning, I could hear Mother in the kitchen. I leapt out of bed. And as I rounded the corner, she was sitting there, smiling, with the cat in her lap. She looked at me and her eyes welled up with tears. 'We were so worried,' she said, 'we thought poor Kitty had run away forever.' [*Pause*] The next day I killed the cat. [*Pause*]

Does that disturb you? I didn't really kill him. God knows why not. I think I couldn't get the washing machine started. What is it about pets that makes them so much more lovable than people? If I licked my genitals, I'd be sent to jail. I suppose it's their dependency on us. It's the closest we ever come to being God. [*Looking out again*] What's more, we out-live them. Most often. They make our own lives seem so much more—eternal. We get to watch hair grow out of our ears. [*Pause*] Summer is so ripe, isn't it? Everything that's going to be, already is. There's nothing more for it to become. [*Pause*] Why are you putting on makeup? [*Pause*] Why don't you let the mortician do that?

Blackout.

SCENE FOURTEEN

*KEMP is out of the room. GRACE, in a flow-
ered hat and light overcoat, and carrying a
purse, goes towards the door. She runs directly
into KEMP. He slowly removes her coat, then
snatches a little piece of paper from her hand.
Looks at it. Looks at her for a long moment.*

KEMP:
I'm concerned about your health these past
few days. It seems to be improving.

*He backs towards her a couple of steps. Fade to
blackout.*

SCENE FIFTEEN

Autumn. There are leaves in the room.
GRACE sits up in bed wearing her hat, clutch-
ing her purse, eating. KEMP enters with a tray
of food. Putting it down in front of her, he goes
to a chair, picks up a newspaper and reads.
Without looking up he speaks to her.

KEMP:

Don't give me that look. You're not going
anywhere. I've got your shopping list. [*Pause*]
Don't you think Christmas wrapping is a little
optimistic? [*Pause, reading*] Oh look. The Post
Office is going on strike. [*Looking up*] I
thought they were on strike. I've yet to
receive my package. I enrolled in a correspondence course. 'Health in the Home.'
[*Pause as she eats*] You eat like a teamster. I
read your letter again. For the seven hun-
dredth time. The one you sent me.
Remember? All that time ago. The one that
brought me here. The one that says 'I'm
dying'? Not that I'm keeping you to your
word. But it's hardly the sort of thing you
change your mind about, is it? Father, the day
he died—had you been there, you'd have
known, of course—the day he died, he was
quite definite. He just sat down in his big old
chair and he said 'I'm going to die now' And
he did. Well, of course, he shot himself, but
still...it seems to me one always knows when

one is dying. It's an instinct everyone has.
Like a sixth sense. One feels the body being
pulled, inexorably, by some force. Some force
outside the body. Like toffee, yanking out a
loose tooth. Well, that's not a terribly good
analogy, but you know what I mean. What's
wrong with the pudding? It's butterscotch.
You like butterscotch. Don't start this, I'm in
the middle of an important theme here,
which, in the end, comes back to you. You
see, it occurred to me the other day, right out
of the blue—well, actually, I got the idea
from this dog. I was watching this dog. In the
park. He found a dirty, maggoty, dead
squirrel in the bushes and he brought it right
up to his owner, and dropped it at her feet.
Well, the woman went completely berserk, of
course. But how was the dog to know. He
probably thought he was doing her a big
favor. And I don't mean to compare your
valiant battle for life to a maggoty squirrel,
but I suddenly thought, 'of course.' You're
doing it for me. You're staying alive for me.
Well, of course, if you want to stay alive,
eating pudding, and whatnot, that's one
thing, but if you're only doing this because
you have some, let's say, notion that I desire
your company, and that's not to say I don't,
but you ought to do what's best for you, and
not worry about me. I'll be fine. [*Pause. She
eats*] I mean, I'll miss you terribly, but I'll—
manage. I just wanted to make that clear. I
don't want you doing anything just to please

32

me. Good. Well, that's settled. [*KEMP reaches into a basket of laundry and begins hanging wet clothes*] Isn't it nice that we can have a frank discussion about these things? Imagine. We hardly even knew each other a few months ago, and now we're carrying on as if we've lived together for years. It's amazing how quickly people can become accustomed to— well, just about anything, really. Come to depend on each other. [*Pause*] Yes. [*Pause*] Of course, I've always lived on my own. Always. Even when I lived at home. Mother never did very much for me, her hands were usually pretty full. What with the cigarette and the glass of scotch. And then, of course, I was packed off to that school. Had you been there, who knows, perhaps you could have intervened on my behalf. She decided I was going to be a priest of all things. Well, what else do you do with an eleven year old trans-vestite? 'It's what all queers grow up to be' she told me, matter-of-factly. It always comes back to me at this time of year, with the first dying leaves, and that gust of cold wind. That cruel stone edifice, and those stern, thin-lipped nuns with their bizarre and inexplicable catechism. But all at once, I felt at home. Not being a Catholic, I had no idea that misery and self-loathing could actually be a religion. I went to confession everyday, stacking up impressive penances. Most were for sins I didn't even commit, but I felt that, given the opportunity, I might. I turned

33

humiliation and prostration into an art form.
I used to spend whole weekends on my
knees. And I even fashioned myself a little
crown of thorns. Well, blackberry bushes. A
vow of silence wasn't enough for me. I took
of vow of paralysis, and didn't move once for
twelve days. Naturally it couldn't last. It was
obvious I wasn't a real Catholic. The rest of
the boys were out shoplifting skin magazines,
while I was punishing myself with a wooden
ruler. The nuns grew increasingly suspicious
of me. Religion is something in the blood,
after all. Piety can be learned, but not true
faith. I didn't believe that anybody cared
about me. Isn't that silly? As it turns out,
nobody even thought about me. [*Pause*]
Anyway—off I was sent. Back home. I spent
the rest of the year employed in the back of
Father's tacky little Magic Shop. He was a
manic depressive. You must have known that.
I was the only one that didn't. I thought it
was normal for people to dig their own
graves in the backyard. But then, I was
wandering around, wearing one of Mother's
bras under my shirt. He used to lock himself
in the garage. For three days at a time. Once,
out of curiosity, I peeked in through the
window, just to see what he was doing. He was
sitting in his car, staring straight ahead, with
his hands on the steering wheel. Motionless.
As if he was driving somewhere in his mind.
Anyway, I snuck into the garage, and quietly
opened the door, and got into the back seat

behind him. For a while, I pretended we were on a journey, just the two of us. I wasn't really happy. I knew we weren't really going anywhere. But I was satisfied. At least we weren't going anywhere together. [*Pause*] Mother had him committed for a while. 'They'll look after him there,' she'd say, 'I can't. I can't even look after myself.' I used to think, 'well fine, but who's looking after me?' She hired me a tutor. I don't know where she found him. This puffy, rum-soaked, Romanian, dwarf with these fat little red hands. He used to slap me on the side of the head whenever I wasn't paying attention. Well, at least we had a relationship. [*Pause*] Why are you looking at me like that? I have to wash my clothes now and again. Do want me to walk around naked? I wasn't expecting to be here for an eternity. The children are all heading back to school, the birds are flying south, the price of stamps is going up once again—everything is in its natural cycle of motion. It's autumn, in case you hadn't noticed! And I have nothing else to wear! So don't look at me like that. I know you think I'm odd. That was clear the one and only time you came to visit. The one and only time! That outfit was my mother's idea. She—she never got over the fact that I was a boy. Neither could I, for that matter. Never quite got the hang of it. All that—muscular thinking. Couldn't catch a ball to save my life. Why would I want to? I'd only have to throw it back again. You can't imagine what

that looked like. [*Pause*] I thought you were a
dream. Arriving a that taxi. Nobody had ever
arrived in a taxi before. You swung your legs
out, onto the sidewalk. One crossed over the
other. You held your hand out, and waited
for the driver. And your hair. When you
stepped out. Your hair. So wild, and beautiful
and black. I just wanted to run up and brush
it. I thought you'd come to rescue me from
my glamourless childhood. Apparently I was
mistaken. You looked at me as if you were
studying a stool sample. I didn't expect you
to love me, you know. I wasn't stupid. But I'd
hoped you might be able to see beyond that
hideous, acne-infested and painfully effemi-
nate thirteen year old in that powder-blue
leisure suit...thing—whatever it was, mincing
around in those buckle shoes—like some
grotesque nightclub act—do you think I
enjoyed playing the accordion for you? Did
you think I chose 'Camptown Races'? None
of it was my idea. Believe me—I had other
plans for my adolescence. I had to get out of
there. I was interesting. Sophisticated
beyond my years. I spoke French. With a
slight Romanian accent, but still. How can
you call yourself an aunt? [*Pause*] Every time
the leaves turn color, I think of you going.
Getting back into a taxi. Forgetting to say
good-bye, and then, oh—and then,
remembering to say good-bye, but forgetting
my name. And then, slinking down into the
seat of that cab as if you weren't even there

anymore. Hurrying off towards some adventure. The Mediterranean or somewhere. There was more than room enough for me in the back of that taxi, you know. I dreamed about you for months. Years. Where are all my letters? You must have got my letters. Of course, that could easily have been the post office. As I say, I'm still waiting for my correspondence course. I'm seriously considering going into medicine. What do you think? [*Pause*] I could do your autopsy, if you like. [*Pause*] Get to know you a little better.

Blackout.

SCENE SIXTEEN

KEMP removes washing from the line, and folds it.

KEMP:

I don't like the word 'survived'. It has too
many perilous connotations. 'Outlived by her
nephew?' 'Outlasted?' Survived. It's more
traditional. Alright, how's this? We'll say that
you left a—a—legacy of love and kindness.
Actually, a legacy of love would be better. It's
more alliterative. Or just a legacy would be—
we don't want to drone on and on about your
attributes—let's just say you left. Of course,
that could sound like a vacation, couldn't it,
but then why would you announce a vacation
in the obituaries? I think it's more precise to
say you're gone. I don't think we should
mince words here. Dead and gone. Nobody's
fooling anybody. You're gone. You're gone,
you're gone. You're dead. You're gone.
Anything else?

Blackout.

SCENE SEVENTEEN

*KEMP at the window with flashlight. It's
night. The room is dark. GRACE is eating
candies. The doorbell rings. KEMP looks out.
He waits.*

KEMP:

Just look at those horrible little Halloween
creatures. Wandering from door to door,
learning how to panhandle. Look at them. I
never went out on Halloween. I wanted to go,
once, as a cardiologist or something, but
Mother wouldn't have it. She wanted me to
go as a ballerina. Of course. [*Pause*] She tried
so hard to turn me into a homosexual. I was
sorry to have disappointed her. I have no
sexuality at all as it turns out. It's my one
saving grace. No one has to rely on my body
for pleasure. Not even me. The idea of geni-
tal contact is—well, let's just say horrifying,
and leave it at that. And the thought that
children can be produced this way is even less
appealing. [*Doorbell, watches*] I think test tubes
and petrie dishes are the way to go in the
future. As for stimulation, there's always a
root canal. The problem is, you see, people
live for sex. It suspends them in a kind of
ether. A daydream. They forget what life
really is. Until the whole viscous and
contorted exercise is over, and then they
remember. Oh, right. I live in hell. But I

never forget. I'm absolutely vigilant about that. Yes, sir. Oh, I've felt an attraction for certain people in the past. Both women and men. Does that shock you? And always inexplicably, of course. Once you take off the mask, they're all the same, aren't they. Needy little children, underneath. [*Doorbell, he watches*] But I've never given in. Because once you lay yourself open like that, certain, let's say, spirits enter you. Mischievous—perhaps even evil—spirits. The body is like a corpse at a wake that you have to watch over. Constantly. Well, I think that's the last of them. We can turn the lights on now. No. Wait. I rather like the darkness. Who knows. I might even see a ghost tonight. [*Lighting his face with the flashlight*] But I'll leave that up to you.

Blackout.

SCENE EIGHTEEN

Morning. GRACE smokes a cigarette, watching out the door. Downstairs, the door slams. She grinds the cigarette into the floor and hurries back into bed. KEMP enters with a bunch of hardware supplies. He stops in the doorway. They eye each other.

KEMP:
I'll be downstairs. Working on some home improvements.

KEMP exits. Music. GRACE watches. Blackout.

SCENE NINETEEN

GRACE lies in bed listening to the sound of hammering and drilling below. She wonders. Continues to knit. Blackout.

SCENE TWENTY

KEMP enters, suddenly, checking on GRACE, and then striking up a casual conversation, as he drags a strange-looking 'machine' into the room, obviously home-made. GRACE watches with interest, as he rigs the contraption around her bed.

KEMP:

I've been thinking about Christmas. Well, I couldn't help it. People are already out shopping. Laying the groundwork for disappointment. Wrapping up their impossible expectations. Tying them with ribbon. People want so much at Christmas time. I don't just mean things, of course. It's as if that one single day could wipe away an entire year in its wake, with a sudden flood of pent-up kindness and goodwill. When I worked at the bank—you remember the bank, auntie. That job I left to come here? I always got a lovely, thoughtful present at Christmas. A frozen turkey. I've always envied turkeys. I can't think of a better way to spend Christmas, really, than to be decapitated and stuffed with chestnuts. While we're on the subject, I think we should discuss the afterlife, don't you? I mean, if you think you're just going to die, and that's it, dust, and you're forgotten, then I can understand your lack of motivation. But this can't be all there is. It just wouldn't be fair, would it? A bit of butterscotch. A few trips to the bathroom. And that's it? [*Pause*] Most religions accept last minute conversions, you know. Mother became some weird thing before she died. And nobody stopped her. The room was filled with these strange people in orange costumes. Quite honestly, I think it was the incense that killed her. But she died happy. The morphine was transcendent. I stood in the corner where she couldn't see me. And then I slipped quietly out of the room. As I walked down the hall, I could hear her voice rising up, over the clicking of finger cymbals. I pretended she was calling for me, but she was calling for more drugs. She didn't even give me the pleasure of forsaking her in the end. Anyway, she found God. So obviously there's hope for anybody. [*Pause*] Right. I've rigged up several options here; as you can see. It's a little controversial, but sometimes we have to think beyond that. I don't want to get into a moral quagmire about it, but isn't it up to the individual to decide how and when their life should come to an end? I don't mean suicide, of course. This isn't about that. It's about—going with the obvious. Once your condition deteriorates to the point where you don't want to drag this out any longer, that you've had about enough of my waiting, that another day would be just one too many, at least you'll have the option. [*Pause*] Here. [*Pause*] It's up to you. [*Pause*] No pressure.

[*Pause*] Pull this one for an electric shock, and this one for a massive blow to the head.

She looks at the rigging, then back at him.

Blackout.

SCENE TWENTY-ONE

*Early evening darkness. GRACE plays
Christmas music from a little music box. She
wipes a tear from her eye.*

Blackout.

Scene Twenty-Two

GRACE stands on one side of the bed, KEMP on the other.

KEMP:

I'm not sure you've quite got the hang of this machine, yet. [*Showing her a little diagram*] I've drawn up a little manual here. See? This one for the shock. This one for a blow to the...

Leaning forward, and studying it for a moment, she pulls the lever on her side. A heavy object comes swinging around behind KEMP, and knocks him into the bed, he wavers, stunned and in shock as the 'electric device' suddenly jolts him. He collapses unconscious. GRACE picks up the diagram. Looks at it. Looks at KEMP. Looks about, a little confused.

Blackout.

SCENE TWENTY-THREE

GRACE looks out the window, as church bells ring. Christmas Eve. KEMP lies in the bed, trying to regain consciousness. Groggily, he rolls himself out of bed, staggers a few steps and collapses. He crawls forward along the floor, reaching the door and pulling himself up along the door frame. Standing, supported by the frame, he turns slowly to GRACE, who is watching him. She smiles.

GRACE:
   Merry Christmas.

   KEMP turns and disappears out the door. GRACE turns back to the window.

   Blackout.

END OF ACT ONE

ACT TWO
SCENE TWENTY-FOUR

Music. A little tree is being decorated, with very make-shift items, by KEMP. GRACE watches, as KEMP steps back and switches on the lights. They look at it for a long moment before KEMP suddenly breaks the mood.

KEMP:
Right. I think we've had enough of that.

Unplugging the·tree, KEMP takes it and tosses it in the closet.

We wouldn't want to belabour the point. [*Looking out at the snow*] Well. [*Brightly*] Merry Christmas. Merry, stupid, horrible, pathetic, rotten, sad, sad, stuff-your-face, let's all feel sorry for the poor for five minutes, and knock back a twenty-six of scotch, Christmas. I could weep for joy. All I can think of is Mother passing out in the gravy.

[*Pause; quietly*] That was the year she bought Father the gun. [*Pause*] I got a nice suitcase. I'm surprised she didn't buy me a ticket somewhere. But that would have suggested a direction on her part. I don't think she wanted me to go anyplace in particular. I think she just wanted me to go. In a way, it was the perfect gift. Ordinarily she didn't even bother. Usually, I was the one. Running around decorating the house, in my red velvet shorts. Wrapping presents for everybody. [*Referring out the window*] Look at her. Still sitting there. [*Pause*] I thought I could make us into a family. Imagine. I had to fill my own stocking on Christmas Eve. It was becoming apparent to me that the best way to find any happiness in life was to invent it. And anyway, I knew from the beginning there was no Santa Claus. Father told me. There's no better way to destroy the magic of childhood than to have a father who's a failed magician. Especially a manic depressive one. Between them, they destroyed every illusion I ever had. And for that I'm grateful, really. What a disappointment life would have turned out to be, otherwise. Still, I would have appreciated being spared the truth for a little while. Perhaps not had my father sitting next to me during that Lassie movie whispering 'the dog trainer is just outside the shot.' [*Pause*] And where were you, by the way? At all those crucial developmental moments? Off on some fabulous adventure, no doubt?

Not even a gift of any kind. Some money in an envelope. An ugly little seashell lamp. Cheap cologne. Anything. All I ever wanted was a sign. A sense, somewhere in the air, of someone, out there, thinking of me.

> GRACE *pulls a little gift, poorly wrapped, out from behind her pillow and hands it to him. KEMP is dumb struck for a moment, and then begins to pace, agitated and completely out of sorts.*

[*Emotional*] How thoughtful. And just what I wanted. Three decades ago. Should we just bury those years out in the back? No. They're ghosts, auntie. Ghosts. Haven't you ever seen a Swedish art film? Everything that never happened between us, never happened. There's no changing any of that with your— with your—sorry, badly wrapped offering. Now comes the atonement, I see. This is how it works. Forgive me. I was under the impression that there was no salvation for any of us, but now I see that in the final hours one is saved by meager half-gestures and long-faced apologies. This is why people are such unconscionable, hateful sinners all their lives, because, in the end, they think they can make themselves into saints. This is what I loathe most about humanity. The refusal of people to account for themselves while they're alive. [*Pause; change of tone*] So, what is it? [*Taking the gift*] No. Don't tell me. [*He

51

turns away from her, shaking the gift, holding it close to him, petting it like a small animal; he turns back to her] It's a lovely little—thing of some kind. Thank you. I'll just keep it— wrapped if that's alright with you. Why spoil Christmas by opening the presents? [*Sincerely*] Besides. I didn't get you anything. Sorry. They couldn't engrave the marble in time.

Blackout.

SCENE TWENTY-FIVE

New Year's Eve. KEMP, looking out the
window. He's slightly inebriated. GRACE is
wearing a party hat. There is noise below in
the street.

KEMP:

Look. They're celebrating the start of the
new year, auntie. Idiots. Imagine. Another
year. They ought to be in mourning like the
rest of us. I suppose they've all made resolu-
tions to improve themselves. To wipe the slate
clean and start all over again. [*Pause; looking
across the street*] I wonder what she's decided?
[*Addressing her*] What have you decided,
madam? What's your heartfelt and instantly-
forgotten resolution? How about taking it
easy next year. Not putting yourself out quite
so much. Look. There's the one-legged man.
My God. I think he's pissed. [*Opening the
window again*] Kicking up a heel, are we? Yes!
Yes! Have a Hoppy New Year! [*KEMP
approaches the bedside table, and surreptitiously
rewires a lamp*] Why promise yourself to be a
better person? You might as well promise
yourself to be a taller person. How does one
ever change? That's what I want to know.
Short of cutting off your own head and stick-
ing it on backwards, what are the options?
You know, I think I'm going to change the
color of my hair this year. If I can't be a

better person, I might as well be a blonder one. [*Pause*] And, of course, I resolve to be a better nephew. That goes without saying. No more of this 'wishing you would drop dead' business, No more 'God, I wonder when she's finally going to kick the bucket.' No. [*Pause, darkly*] No more wishing.

GRACE blows a little horn.

No more wondering.

As KEMP looks at her, a fade to black.

SCENE TWENTY-SIX

KEMP, now in a bad blonde wig, enters nervously, with a tray of food, which he places carefully in front of GRACE.

KEMP:
  I've made you a special pudding.

  KEMP casually makes his way to the phonograph, putting on a record. GRACE falls asleep, as KEMP approaches her. He picks up a pillow, holding it over her. GRACE wakes, looks about. He turns off the record.

Why aren't you eating your butterscotch?
[*She picks up a spoon*] No! Don't! Wait.
[*Grabbing the pudding from her*] There might be something wrong with this. What are you accusing me of? I told you that I read things far too quickly to ever understand them. 'Instant Pudding' looks a little like 'Ant Poison,' when you run it altogether like that.

He exits, strangely. Blackout.

SCENE TWENTY-SEVEN

*Night. Moonlight lights the room. KEMP
stands off to one side, running a scarf through
his hands, staring at GRACE, as she counts
her days.*

KEMP:
I think I might be going mad. I don't know
what makes me do certain things and
prevents me from doing others. [*Pause*] I
remember, when I was a teenager, I would
sneak out late at night, and sit across the
street, watching my house. As if I was guard-
ing it against myself. I wanted to kill my
parents. I wanted to bludgeon them to death
with a tire iron, and then burn the house
down with gasoline. Why didn't I? [*Pause*]
Why didn't I? Maybe there's some good in
me, after all. [*He cries, stops*] No. Now I
remember. I'm a coward. I was afraid of the
dark until I was eighteen. I suppose I kept
hoping that you might come along and turn
on the light.

She reaches over, to turn on the lamp.

No. Wait. Don't turn it on.

She turns it on anyway. KEMP rushes to turn it back off, which sends a surge of electric shock through him; taking his hand away, he sits motionless, smoldering.

That was oddly satisfying. [*Pause*] I can actually feel my lips turning blue. [*Pause*] If you don't die soon, I think it's going to kill me.

The lights fade to black.

Scene Twenty-Eight

KEMP, at the window, holding a piece of rope and wearing a pair of black gloves.

KEMP:

[*Turning in*] Right. I'm not sure how to say this. I'm sorry if it looks a little like impatience on my part. But I'm not thinking about the year gone by. I'm thinking about the years ahead. You don't seem to be on a very tight schedule. And this is not how I envisioned spending the rest of my life. Well, to tell you the truth, I don't know how I envisioned spending the rest of my life. But it's almost certain that you didn't fit into the plans. So I've made up my mind.

Pause. Suddenly, and violently, he attacks himself with the rope, trying to strangle himself, as GRACE tries to intervene by hitting him with a pillow.

GRACE:

No.

KEMP:

What are you doing? What are you doing? Get away, for God's sake. Get away.

They struggle for a bit, until the doorbell

sounds. Suddenly, they both stop, looking at each other. KEMP makes his way over to the window and looks out. He looks at GRACE

It's the police.

Blackout.

SCENE TWENTY-NINE

GRACE looks out the window. KEMP re-enters.

KEMP:
I don't think they suspected anything. I was very natural. [*Noticing he is still wearing the gloves and holding the rope*] Oh, my God. Do you think they noticed? Why would they? They didn't come for me, anyway. They came about the woman across the street. Asked if we knew anything about her. She's a neighbour, I said, of course we don't. [*Looking out the window*] Apparently she's dead. Imagine. Apparently she's been dead for a very long time. Poor woman. No wonder she looked like a corpse. They said that she was clutching a faded old photograph in her hand. Isn't that sad? A little boy with the mumps. Probably some relative who never bothered to...

Pause. Slowly, KEMP turns to look at GRACE. He looks out the window again, back at GRACE. In his mind, now, he calmly reviews the entire year. His eyes moving about the room, here and there, seeing himself in every situation. Again, he looks at GRACE, out the window, and then back to GRACE.

KEMP:
> For a moment there, I got the most awful, sickening feeling that I was in the wrong house.

GRACE:
> Oh?

> *GRACE turns away and putters, as KEMP follows.*

KEMP:
> But, of course, that would mean we weren't even related.

GRACE:
> Well, not to each other. No.

> *She looks at him sheepishly. He opens his mouth to speak. He faints.*

> *Blackout.*

SCENE THIRTY

*KEMP stands at the window. GRACE stands
opposite, looking at him.*

KEMP:

They can't even get her into the back of that
station wagon. They're propping her upright
in the seat. Oh my God. I've never seen rigor
mortis like that. This is awful.

*KEMP watches the car disappear down the
street. He walks, solemnly, to the door, without
looking a GRACE. He picks up his suitcase.
He stops. He turns. Pause.*

There's little to say at this point that wouldn't
be an understatement. The idea that you
were my aunt was unbearable. The idea that
you're not is unforgivable. [*Pause, suddenly
slapping himself on the side of the head*] WHAT
have I DONE? WHAT have I DONE? WHERE
have I BEEN? It's the WRONG ADDRESS!!
WHEN will I LEARN to pay ATTENTION!?
To PAY...ATTENTION!! [*Stopping abruptly,
advancing on GRACE*] I've been nowhere.
Nowhere. Looking after...no one. Stuffing
you with pudding and keeping you alive. For
what? If I didn't think you could charge me
with false pretenses, I'd charge you with
fraud. Don't you think it would have been
easier if you'd just stabbed me the head with

a barbeque fork? Isn't my life stupid and pointless enough, without you underlining it in red pencil? Why didn't you say something?

GRACE:
I was glad of a visit.

KEMP:
Visit? This was a hostage-taking. You trapped me in this house for a year, and blindfolded me to the truth. Look. I realize what desperation there is in loneliness. But if a person so keenly desires the company of others, I think a home of some kind might be more suitable.

GRACE:
Wouldn't you be happier here?

A momentary pause. KEMP makes his way to the door, speechless. We hear him descend the stairs and close the door. GRACE turns and looks about the room, as the lights fade to black.

Scene Thirty-One

*GRACE stands at the window, looking out.
Sighs. Returns to her bed, and picks up her
knitting. She looks at it, sighs, as the lights
fade to black.*

Scene Thirty-Two

GRACE sits on the side of the bed, knitting. She holds up the sweater.

GRACE:
Almost finished.

She sighs. She continues knitting.

Fade to black.

SCENE THIRTY-THREE

*Moonlight fills the room. The sweater finished,
GRACE hangs it in the middle of the room. She
returns to her bed, and sits, looking at the
sweater. She smiles as if she's being visited by
an old friend. The lights fade.*

SCENE THIRTY-FOUR

*Night. GRACE lies in her bed. The sweater is
hung in the middle of the room. There is a
light rap at the door downstairs. We hear the
door creak open. Close. Footsteps, ascending the
stair. A long shadow is cast, as KEMP enters a
little into the room.*

KEMP:
Why were you lying here in the dark?

GRACE:
It's the middle of the night.

KEMP:
Oh. Right. So it is. [*Pause*] I was sitting across
the street. On my suitcase. Just now.
Wondering—why I was sitting across the
street on my suitcase. I thought I should
come up and say goodbye. I owe you at least
that much. After all I've said and done. It was
pretty awful. But then, I thought you were a
relative. [*About to go, he pauses, considers*] I,
uh...I'd go back to the bank, but I'm no
longer part of the fiduciary trust, you might
say. [*Pause*] The day I got that letter, I went
straight up to the manager, and I said 'my
aunt is dying. I'll need a couple of days off.'
A couple of years would have been more
precise. But never mind. He didn't even look
up from his work. He said 'I'm afraid it's bad

timing.' It's the sort of thing he always said. I
didn't even really think twice about it. Just
headed back downstairs. You know, when you
first start working at the bank they like to
welcome you to the family. They even gave
me a card on my birthday. It was always the
wrong day, but still...a card. 'Best wishes from
your savings and loan family.' I was
really...very moved. I felt I was actually a part
of something. Imagine. [*Pause*] But when I
got to the bottom step I sort of sat down, I
guess. Hanging onto the rail. Just sort of...sat.
In a kind of thick-headed fog. I looked over
at my desk, without me in it. I suddenly
realized what 'bad timing' my death would be
for the bank. Not sad. Not tragic. Just...inop-
portune. No, I thought. When I go, I think
I'd like them all to feel the profound loss of
something.

GRACE:
It's not very nice to be unwanted.

KEMP:
Well, I definitely would have been wanted.
But I was in such a hurry, I absconded with
the suitcase, before I'd actually put the
money in it. Does that surprise you?

GRACE:
Someone must be looking out for you, dear.

KEMP:

No one's looking out for anyone, I'm afraid. I was staring up at this house. I couldn't help notice how lonely it looked in the lamplight. I thought, You're a constipated, old woman. You so much as sneeze and they're stoking up the crematorium fires. That's what the world is like, now. No sense of obligation. You see some old geezer on the bus, you think 'my God, he's taking up a perfectly useful seat.' Some old doll, fishing through her change purse. All these wrinkled up and forgotten old souls. Who's going to bring them their puddings? A fat, odious, leering nurse, with a hypodermic needle? Some scrub-nosed lawyer with a mortgage buy-back scheme? Where is human compassion gone? That's what I'd like to know. Who considers you an obligation?

GRACE:

I think I'd rather be an amaryllis.

KEMP:

In a better world, there would be somebody, here, at your side.

GRACE:

There is.

Blackout.

SCENE THIRTY-FIVE

GRACE half-dozes, holding a hand of cards.
KEMP sits near to her, holding a hand of
cards, trying to decide what to discard, occa-
sionally peeking at her cards.

KEMP:

I was just thinking. I might be charged with
criminal negligence. I mean, I don't know if
there's a law against letting your own aunt rot
in a chair for a year while you sit and mock
her from across the street, but if there isn't,
don't you think there should be? [*Pause*]
Maybe they'll include my time here as part of
my sentence. Go fish. [*KEMP helps play her
hand*] Bad luck. My turn. [*He plays again*]
Look at that. I win again. [*Pause*] What's
wrong with you? Your attitude has been so
negative in the past few days. Alright. Fine.
Let's have another round, then. Alright. Let's
not. I don't know what you want. I'll make
you some more butterscotch pudding. Fine.
I'm going to work on my memoirs, then.

He sits, holds a pen motionless, to a piece of
paper. He looks around the room, waiting for
the muse to strike him. The sound of children

I find it impossible to concentrate in here.
[*Going over to the window and opening it*]

Someone is going to throw that ball right
through a window.

*Suddenly a ball flies through the window, and
lands in his arms. KEMP considers, then
throws it out, wildly out the window. Watches.
The sound of glass shattering. KEMP turns
back into the room.*

KEMP:
There. What did I tell you? [*Sensing her
fading*] Are you sure you wouldn't like to go
to the park? I could show you the man with
the wooden leg. He's a little nuts but he's
actually quite harmless. He stepped on a land
mine. Did you know that? Not in the park, of
course. In the war. I don't know which one.
Some war. He said he just happened to be in
the wrong place at the wrong time. I said I
know how you feel. Well, I've never lost a leg,
but in a way we're all hobbling around, aren't
we? Missing little bits and pieces of ourselves.
[*Pause*] That's rather good.

Sits to write. Stops.

You know what he told me? He said that
when he first lost his leg, he couldn't be
convinced that it was gone. He kept reaching
down to scratch his foot. Isn't that something? He says he still, occasionally, feels a
kind of tingling sensation. How ironic.
[*Studying his legs*] I don't feel any attachment

71

to my legs whatsoever. [*Considering*] Do you suppose when we're gone, there's a sense of us missing, in the air, somewhere? A kind of tingling sensation?

GRACE reaches over and touches him.

Oh. Why did you touch me? My goodness. You frightened me. What on earth is wrong? [*Realizing*] Oh, I see. Oh.

He pats her hand, and then pulls his arm away.

Yes. Affection. Lovely. [*Pause*] Affection [*Pause*] Yes, well. Fortunately, one doesn't receive it very often. I can never quite think of an appropriate reciprocal gesture. [*Pause*] Would twenty dollars be too much?

GRACE:
The sweater. [*Pause*] It's for you.

KEMP:
That? Oh. This is...it's really unnecessary. For me? [Going over to the sweater] Oh look. It's even got little...sleeves and everything.

GRACE has fallen asleep. She snores a little.
KEMP holds the sweater with affection, and
then drops it. He walks over to GRACE as she
sleeps. Studies her hair for a moment. He takes
a brush beside the bed and begins gently
brushing. Music. Blackout.

SCENE THIRTY-SIX

*KEMP plays an accordion, picking out notes,
in an effort to revive a dying companion.
GRACE is half-conscious. A few leaves fall.*

KEMP:

[*Suddenly stopping*]. I've just had a brilliant
idea. We could miss winter entirely if we went
south. If you're just going to just lay about all
day, I might as well be pushing you down
some Mediterranean promenade. [*Thinking*]
How do you say 'pudding' in Spanish? Never
mind. We'll go to France. I can order better
there. What do you think? Well, I think it's a
wonderful idea. Would you like to go to
France?

GRACE:

[*Feebly*]. I'm sorry to interrupt, but would you
excuse me, please?

*She dies, which KEMP fails to notice, as he
begins packing things for the trip.*

KEMP:

What? Excuse you? Oh, no. No you are not
excused, Madame. You are coming whether
you like it or not. We are loading ourselves
into the back of that taxi and we're gone!
Mon Dieu! I'm so excited. I've never been

anywhere, except back and forth across this
stupid country.

*Pause, as KEMP sees her. He lifts her hand a
little, then drops it.*

KEMP:

Oh. Yes, well. I see. In that case, you're
excused.

*He holds his head for a moment, not knowing
quite what to do.*

[*Suddenly continuing to pack*] No. No, you're
not excused. You're not. We have other plans.
Other plans, Madame! I'm going to buy
myself a white linen suit. And some white
penny-loafers. Of course, in France, they
would be centime-loafers, wouldn't they? And
I'll introduce you to everyone as my aunt, if
that's alright. You might as well be. Besides, I
happen to like you. In my own way. I hope it
doesn't embarrass you to hear that. It embar-
rasses me to say it, but anyway, it's true. You
really should have been my aunt all along. I
think it was right that I came here, somehow.
And, let's face it, she wouldn't be much of a
traveling companion at this point. But you
and me, we can make up for all that. All of it.
Forget the butterscotch. There's going to be
creme caramel. And by the way, it's not
'excuse me.' It's 'excuse moi.' [*Stopping*] Oh,

75

my God. What's the French for suppositories?
Don't worry. I'll pack you some.

*He picks up the sweater. He looks at it for a
moment, then puts it on. It is very tiny.*

Excuse you! What kind of manners are these,
anyway? Dropping off stupidly, in the middle
of the afternoon.

*He stands for a moment, pulling at the sweater,
and making himself fit into it. He marches
over to GRACE.*

[*Angrily*] It's too fucking small!

*He sits beside her. Looks at her for a moment.
Without emotion, he lifts one of her hands and
puts the brush in it, combing his hair. He puts
the hand down. And removes the sweater.*

KEMP:
Just like all the rest. You leave like all the rest.
Why couldn't we all go at the same time?
Then we wouldn't have to watch each other
die.

Blackout.

SCENE THIRTY-SEVEN

Music. Another evening. Outside it snows.
GRACE is gone. KEMP stands in the middle
of the room, jacket on, suitcase nearby, dump-
ing the contents of an urn into a plant pot. He
inserts a bulb, and sets the pot in the bed. Picks
up his suitcase, and goes to the door. Opens it.
Snow falls. He closes the door, puts his suitcase
down, and slowly walks to the bed. Picks up the
plant pot. Looks at it. Puts it down again. He
walks over to a chair. Sits, waiting. The snow
continues to fall, as the lights fade.

THE END